Heaven's Secret Garden

Copyright © 2018 Shanda E. Sanders

This is a work of fiction. Names, characters,

places and incidents either are the product

of the author's imagination or are used

fictitiously, and any resemblance to any

actual persons, living or dead, events, or

locales is entirely coincidental.

This book was printed in the United States

of America.

Heaven's Secret Garden

Table of Contents

Book Summary

Heaven's Secret Garden is a collection of

short stories for people of all ages. The

stories are designed to help people make

better choices and provide them with a

monopoly of avenues to stretch their faith

and their imagination.

Inner Beauty will challenge your faith with

a moving word from the author to never

lose hope even when the odds are against

you, you can still come out as a "true winner".

Day of Emancipation will touch your heart

and intrigue your minds as two orphans

raised by the state grow closer to God

and to each other. As one vastly approaches

his day of emancipation, will the two have

to say goodbye?

Lady Turquoise is filled with an adventurous

turn of events that will leave you in awesome

wonder until the very end. This story will

boggle the mind of young readers and

leave you baffled about the spirit world…

the world we never see, but we know that it

does exist.

Mixed Signals is a science fiction that will

teach us all how to go the extra mile,

appreciate and respect others who are

not only different from us, but it teaches us

about the power of sacrifice when we

are in need of a helping hand. It is the

demonstration of unity when a rescue

mission puts them in potential danger

to help save a fallen ship and its crew get

back on their feet after a calamity struck

causing their ship to be damaged beyond

repair.

These short stories are filled with lessons

to be learned that your children will share

with their children someday. Heaven's Secret

Garden always has a story to share that will

help anyone with an open mind grow and

mature spiritually, socially, and intellectually

in today's world.

~Shanda E. Sanders~

Heaven's Secret Garden: Shanda E. Sanders

ABOUT THE AUTHOR: Testimony of Faith

Shanda has been writing her way out of the

storms of life since early childhood. However,

she was only seven when one of her instructors

informed her that she had an extraordinary gift

inside of her that would some day blossom and

open up major doors for her in the area of

journalism should she pursue her passion

for writing. Philippians 4:13

Heaven's Secret Garden is a storybook for all ages

that the whole family will enjoy...

AUTHOR BIOGRAPHY: Shanda E. Sanders

Shanda spent years as a teacher, child

advocate, minister of music, and now a

published author who faced the everyday

challenges of life as a Christian who dealt

with different facets of abuse and neglect

inside and outside the church. Shanda

daringly overcame several illnesses and

temporary disabilities as a child simply by

using the power of her imagination lodged

deeply in her faith in God. Not to mention,

the persuasiveness of the love and care

that surrounded her daily. While enduring

a mental psychosis in her young adulthood,

Shanda decided that the only way out was

to write down everything that came to mind.

And so she did, which led to several

unpublished diaries that she reflects upon

from time to time. In her healing process,

Shanda found her release in the joy of

writing and did so successfully with the

support of many who she reached out to

with simple poems, letters of love and

admiration, and short stories that helped

to aid her in her healing process of forgiving

herself, others, and God as well. She

knows the struggles of what it means to live

life as a survivor, as she pushes others not

to shoulder life as a victim but seek to

overcome the trials of life with a renewed

sense of faith. She finally understands

what it means to be an over comer by faith.

Now living a healthy and whole life in God,

both reassured and reclaimed in her level

of spiritual growth and development, Shanda

reaches out to those who are on the journey,

but have lost their way. In one of her books,

Shanda was inspired by her own personal

experience to use her own name as part of

her healing process. There are no illustrations

within the books because she hopes to

empower others through the art of their own

imagination of Heaven's Secret Garden.

Philippians 4:13

About the Book: Heaven's Secret Garden

Heaven's Secret Garden is based on the

biblical scripture from Philippians 4:13.

These stories of faith will elevate your spirit

and open your mind to the possibility that

you can do all things through Christ which

strengthens you in Heaven's Secret Garden.

~Shanda E. Sanders~

Heaven's Secret Garden:

In loving memory of:

My Sister in Christ, Cassie

John 14

Acknowledgments

To All of the Timeless Treasures in

Heaven's Secret Garden:

…thank you so much.

1 Peter 1:15-17

Dedication: *Philippians 4:13*

To my blessed mother, Mary, for never

diminishing in her prayers for me.

To my daddy, for teaching me the joy

of reading. To my daughter, Alliyah

for never diminishing in your faith

that together we will complete

this project. To my precious baby girl,

Shariyah, and all of my family,

I love you so much.

~Shanda E. Sanders~

HEAVEN'S SECRET GARDEN: INNER BEAUTY

In two different dimensions, two women fight

for the same mythical cause called "freedom"

on one side of the world, a young lady connected

to images of both worlds, the natural world and

the spirit world, by means of a suicide attempt that

ultimately left the darkness and the light disputing

over to whom her soul truly belongs to. Nevertheless,

death, in her eyes, seemed like a gift, and life was

an undeserving reward. She finds herself seen by the

unseen, and touched by the untouchable . . . she had

a voice in a place where souls were never heard. She

used her gift wisely and discretely. never wanting

anyone to be as she was . . . trapped in between

two worlds, she worked in the shadows of death's

open door to complete what they could not finish,

guiding them to the light that was meant for them

alone, and rendering them to a newfound imitation

of freedom . . . a life they never had to relive . . . a life

they never knew . . . creating dreams that they never

dreamed were possible. while on the other side of an

undiscovered world, "the spirit world", a place that

only exist beyond the scope of where one's faith in the

human ability ends . . . and their secure faith in a god

that they have never seen begins, she tries aimlessly

to hold onto every spirit that crosses her path to

rebuild a world that she destroyed through means of

the curse of becoming an angry god. However, looking

beyond what you see in her eyes, and into her spirit

you will find that this curse is just what it is and has

never come close to defining her true nature at all.

She has been the only true sign of life in a world much

like a desert, a ghost town, or a backstreet alley for

as long as forever came into existence. She refuses to

allow an undeserving curse by another angry god to

defer her dreams any longer. She rebuilds her world

slowly but surely. She has separated the grains of

every spiritual being and created a world that would

define their next transition into a future world . . .

a world that most of them would never see due to

her desire to never let go of a world that she felt she

could never leave. on the other side of the world,

the other young lady had always detected someone

inside of herself but separate from her true self, in

the reflection of her mirror, in the pond at the park

or her waterfront yard, at the ice rink, in her store

front window, and so many other places . . . she knew

there existed a twin, a clone of her true self that was

in a place beyond her reflection . . . desperate to be

reunited, she acknowledges every spiritual being

that comes into her presence, hoping that she will

know what the true meaning of "wholeness" is for

her one day. For she, exist in a body, who has a spirit,

but dwells in the darkness of where her soul once

lived. She manages a bookstore, and a side shop that

restores antiques . . . where she often experiences

her visitations. She never leaves her world to reunite

them to their place of destiny. for her, it would be as

though she has chosen sides . . . she knows that

the only answer and guarantee she has of never

crossing over and leaving all she knows behind is to

stay positioned where time has left her and somehow

forgotten her name. Disturbing time, in a world full of

"timeless reflections", could either restore balance to

a world that fell into the hands of time or reunite her

with the time that forced her into her place of being

as she knows it to be. However, one day she looked

in the mirror and only saw a warped image of her

reflection gone badly. The image puzzled her all day.

She was out and about, working at the shops, and

running her daily errands, when she lost her balance

and disappeared into a distorted image of the world

she had lived in for so long. The people looked the

same, but there was something very different. She

ran back to the store and everything was as it should

be. But only there . . .

for outside of those store front doors laid a whole

other world that she had never seen. Longing for

answers, she locked herself in her store and searched

through every book for a way to explain to her what

was happening. But every time she opened a book and

read, the characters would literally come alive, only

in spirit form at first . . . but when she spoke to them

and acknowledged their presence, they manifested

into human form. She didn't understand . . . but it

became more and more clear that she was being

led by the imagination of another being . . . a

powerful being thrusting her into a world that she

didn't want to know. Or at least wasn't ready to

know. The store was packed with every book that

she read through . . . so she put the books away

thinking the characters would simply disappear. But

they did not leave. They didn't understand what

was happening to them and they wanted answers,

but she had none.

Shanda said, "Quickly, quickly, you must leave.

You must leave the store now. I don't have time

to explain . . . I don't know how to explain . . . oh,

never mind, I will explain it to you later." (Pushing

everyone out of the store)

She knew she had a lot of work to do.

Shanda begins to think out loud. Now researching

this phenomenon in my books and using my

imagination has caused things to manifest that are

unexplainable to the human mind. Let me see, I

know. I will look it up on the computer.

But every time she clicked on something it would

come to be in the realm of her reality. Or was it her

reality? No, there was another source behind all of

this. The store was packed once again but this time she

was smart. She only clicked on doctors, scientist, and

spiritual leaders who could leave her with some type

of explanation for all of these strange happenings.

But still no answers that satisfied her. She heard an

unfamiliar noise in the store. She walked in slowly as

she was mesmerized by the most astonishing light. But

the light recognized her level of glory and dissipated.

"Wait", she said, I need to . . .

She looked down and the light had left behind a

beautiful, little trinket box. It looked empty so she

closed it up and laid it on her desk. She walked away

and started searching the store in hope of more

answers. But to no avail . . . suddenly she heard a still

small voice that said . . .

The voice said, "Look in the box".

She ignored the voice because she had just looked

into the box, which was empty. Later, she picked up

the box and decided to go home.

Finally, a place I recognize, she stated.

She was home. She dropped the box and a small

golden key fell out of it. She looked puzzled but

she picked up the box and the key . . . she had no

idea what the key was for. But it was late so she

went to bed. She put the key under her pillow. She

quickly fell asleep. as she slept, she navigated into

a world of words . . . it was a warning that led into

the world that she was oh too familiar with . . .

Spiritual Brainstorms

excellence, ambition, courage, confidence,

extraordinarily gifted, composer in her own right,

loving, loved in return, universally-known for

helping those in need, phenomenal memorization,

world renown, goal oriented, maintaining reign

and upward range in every aspect of my life,

supportive, saved, sanctified, holy ghost filled,

fire baptized, encouraging and encouraged daily,

brilliant in Christ, energetic and self-motivator,

responsible, clean, respectful and respected,

people friendly, reliable source with reliable

sources, trustworthy,

God-fearing, truthful, honest, unspeakable joy,

always employed with pay, volunteer when

necessary, values and morally correct, assertive,

aggressive when necessary, puts God first, mother

second, and teacher always . . . interchangeable,

musically inclined, author of salvation, healed,

priceless education, forgiving, broken in

spirit and proven in word, thought, and deed,

unique and unpredictable, full of grace and mercy,

rich in spirit, committed to truth, and honesty,

competitive spirit, confident in the Jesus in me.

I believe that you should only

be taught by those who can live the life that they

teach and preach about. I haven't met a one yet

that can stand by the stones they throw at other

people because the truth of the matter is,

if I threw...the voice continued.

Then the voice shouted loudly.

Do not enter my dimension if your spirit can't survive

the way of correction that has been designed for

you. What's worse? Don't start a fire that you

can't put out or that you can't stay in yourself.

It was a message from the other side and I had the

key of words to unlock the door to this mystery.

She woke up and grabbed a picture image of the

words she saw in her dream. She wrote the words

down and immediately endured the journey that led

her to the other side of this mystery. She had no clue

how to get back. Honestly, the journey was so

enlightening and powerful to her that she reached

a stage in the words that caused her to never want

to leave.

But she knew she had to go back because she had

souls to save and spiritual awakenings to account

for on the other side. Once again, she sacrificed her

place of happiness for beings she did not know.

She walked out her destiny so that her heart could

lead her home, back to a chaotic world searching for

answers to a strange phenomenon that was sweeping

across many nations.

She embarks upon a small still voice in the shadows

of her being.

Be careful of how you enter her grand foyer of

master pieces, crucified flesh, corrupted dominions,

decapitated scenes built on hopes of unfinished

dreams, so many things undone, and a distorted truth

of things unseen. She knows, she saw . . . the things

she never spoke of, became your circle of undefined

law. Obviously, you used the key to get in but when

her thoughts became yours and her skin becomes

your skin…can you use the same key to get out the sin

that you took in? So now . . . go ahead and brag about

you holding the key but from the fingertip to the toe

nail you scream silently to be set free. I told you it's

safer in the garden on the other side. For here, once

you enter in, I can no longer be your friend. I have

to show you what is to come and what shall be your

end. Don't blame me. There was no welcome mat

as you can see. The truth is no key was ever designed

for you to break free.

Who are you? How did you know that I had

the key? Shanda asked the voice.

The voice vocalized everything she asked

musically.

"Who are you? How did you know that I had

the key?", the voice echoed.

"I recognize that voice. Sing to me again.

Please. Oh, please. Your voice . . . your

spirit. I am so far away from home, Shanda

whimpered."

The voice fades into the atmosphere. She starts

to cry. The crying reaches a level of wailing

that she never knew was inside of her. Softly,

she begins to moan and groan in distress.

Out of nowhere, she hears a faint voice that

musically pulls her out of her distress.

(Song)

Heaven's Secret Garden…

we're alone in his presence.

Heaven's Secret Garden…

divine worship with thee.

O, how I love to sing in His presence.

Heaven's Secret Garden…

He alone deserves the reverence.

In Heaven's Secret Garden,

divine worship with thee.

She responds quickly to the voice and they

began to vocalize musically together.

"I need your divine presence, said Shanda."

"And, I need your name, said the voice."

"I see your face and I hear your holy name, O Lord.

I bow in your divine presence and I submit to your

holy name." Shanda said to the voice."

"Where two or three are gathered together

in my name, I shall be in the midst.

We can now come together

in divine fellowship

with thanksgiving

and praise on our lips

in Heaven's Secret Garden." The voice stated to Shanda.

"I love to sing in your divine presence

in Heaven's Secret Garden.

We honor you with divine worship

where shall we find thee." Shanda spoke internally

to the voice.

"In Heaven's Secret Garden

on my knees, the voice answered."

"Then ye shall find me

upon my face in prayer as well, thought Shanda."

The voice said to her, "Have I ever let you

down?"

Shanda said, "It's your music that always

rescues me."

"And it's your spirit that brings me peace and

refuge, said the voice."

Shanda thought inwardly, you are my match

in the spirit.

Shanda asked the voice, "Where am I?"

The voice responds, "You are in Heaven's

arena, my child. You are here to unlock the

mysteries within the heart of God. I have seen your

level of worship in the spirit. You are the last key.

We cannot move on without you. We've been called

to a greater level of worship. But you, my

child, have an even greater calling upon

your life. Are you ready to fly?"

"Fly? Are you kidding me?" Shanda said

jokingly.

The voice said, "Come on, I will take you

there."

Shanda said in awesome wonder, "The

light . . . it's soooo beautiful."

"It's here because of you. The beauty of the

light is immolating out of you. This light . . .

well, it is you, said the voice."

Shanda said, "You mean all of these years . . .

all of this time. All of the times I have

witnessed the beauty of this light and led

so many into it...I can't believe that all of this time,

I have been running from myself. So, you mean to

tell me all of the spiritual beings I have led into this

beautiful array of light live within me."

The voice triumphantly spoke, "Yes, my child and

you will simply be walking into your own being,

your true self. Many dimensions in

Heaven's Secret Garden will stand in awe of your

arrival . . . your wondrous glory." "You mean I

will finally know what it means to be whole…

to be complete? But how can this be…?"

The voice quietly sings . . . we wait for you,

we're not in a hurry.

Shanda asked, "So what's it like…on the other

side, I mean?"

The voice stated, "Well, we all have different

experiences as we pass through the light.

Every time for me, it seems different, yet more

and more peaceful. We call it for the lack of a better

word "The Light of Glory" and now the time

has come for you to show us the way. Your

way . . . a way that we have never traveled or

seen. When you go beyond Heaven's arena

you will embark upon several entry ways."

"But which way shall I go?" Shanda asked the

voice.

"Stand still and wait, said the voice."

Shanda said, "Wait . . . for what?"

The voice spoke in the distance. "Wait . . .

for the music. Your spirit will breathe

the awakening of a new song. It will be a level of

worship your spirit has never known.

It will be the key that unlocks the right

door for you. When the door opens your

steps will be ordered by the words of your

new song. Everything you need will be at

your fingertips once you and the words

to your new song are on one accord. At

first, it will be like a computer simulation.

Nothing around you will seem real but

you'll adjust." The voice spoke clearly.

Shanda said, "Hold it . . . wait a minute. I

thought you said that you didn't know

what I was to expect."

The voice stated, "It is no longer I that responds

to you . . . but the presence within me.

She is aware of your presence. She is awaiting

your arrival. You must enter into the light

now. The gate is open . . . please, don't let us miss

our turn at destiny."

Shanda recognized that she had entered into a

new realm of the spirit and it was necessary

for her to be issued a new

name so the voice will recognize her spirit

in Heaven's arena. Her new name . . . Journey.

The perfect name for a new start in Heaven's Arena.

So, Journey feeling unconnected to the voice

inside her spirit slowly walked into the light.

And so it was, she became the true essence

of the light of glory and as for us, she is the

light of which our journey shall have no

end. For it is because of Heaven's pure light,

that we will never know darkness.

Of course, curious as to where the light had led them,

still the journey never ends for some of us but a light of

poetic justice awaits us all as we walk in the glorious

creation of Heaven's covenant of peace:

Isn't it enough that I gave up eternity

now there's only you and there's no me.

Do I have to give up my soul

to prove I love you so?

How much more do you require of thee?

There's only you…there is no me.

Entering in at the west gate of your love

love's eternal embrace,

purity, grace, and eternal airwaves

stages of a spiritual death

only an extension of my world will know of.

follow me now into Heaven's Secret Garden,

where the waterfalls become your ocean

of purifying destiny. . . before I become

you and you become me.

A rainbow of clarity

I will endow upon thee, in the purification

of Heaven's Secret Garden, your never-ending

heavenly mansion of hope,

serenity, love, mercy, and peace . . .

an illumination of "the heart of God"

as solid as the rock enticing the rivers and

streams . . .that now live ever-so boldly within me.

Like Heaven's pure light that now pours

heavily into my very soul (ever-flowing),

the stillness of the night...an internal glow

Impregnating outwardly...with Heaven's glory as my

omnipresent entry way.

Thank you now for the face I see

of the eternal God that lives inside of me.

For grains of sand, that is Heaven's pure gold

rivers and streams of God's anointing oil.

Shimmering playgrounds of Heaven's open

door glittering pearls, diamonds, rubies of red,

and yes, there is more.

Shhh! You never heard it from me...no, not one

word of this must ever be spoken. For ears have

not heard nor eyes have ever seen.

You are an eternal overflow of the mysterious

flight into Heaven's Secret Garden . . .

inflaming my soul with hope of an

everlasting tomorrow of eternal glory

forevermore. Now Glory, a minister of

the prophetic testimony (test being trial,

mony meaning song) in you is free to tell

your story of "Heaven's Secret Garden"

and "Heaven's belle" which means

Heaven's beauty in French. It is true.

Le ciel est magnifique. Heaven is beautiful.

Heaven's Secret Garden

Inner Beauty

I can do all things through Christ which strengthens me. Philippians 4:13

The Challenge(s):

_____
_____
_____
_____
_____
_____
_____
_____
_____
_____
_____
_____
_____
_____
_____
_____
_____
_____
_____
_____
_____
_____
_____
_____
_____
_____
_____
_____
_____
_____
_____
_____Philippians 4:13

Heaven's Secret Garden

I can do all things through Christ which strengthens me. Philippians 4:13

The Experience(s):

_____
_____
_____
_____
_____
_____
_____
_____
_____
_____
_____
_____
_____
_____
_____
_____
_____
_____
_____
_____
_____
_____
_____
_____
_____
_____
_____
_____
_____
_____Philippians 4:13

Heaven's Secret Garden

I can do all things through Christ which strengthens me. Philippians 4:13

The Victory:

_____
_____
_____
_____
_____
_____
_____
_____
_____
_____
_____
_____
_____
_____
_____
_____
_____
_____
_____
_____
_____
_____
_____
_____
_____
_____
_____
_____
_____
_____
_____
_____
_____Philippians 4:13

Heaven's Secret Garden

I can do all things through Christ which strengthens me. Philippians 4:13

Scripture(s) and Prayer(s): That Brought Healing and Strength to Your Experience

_____
_____
_____
_____
_____
_____
_____
_____
_____
_____
_____
_____
_____
_____
_____
_____
_____
_____
_____
_____
_____
_____
_____
_____
_____
_____
_____
_____
_____
_____Philippians 4:13

HEAVEN'S SECRET GARDEN:

DAY OF EMANCIPATION

Emancipated from the only life they have ever

known, Gabrielle and Daniel can now gravitate

to a place in time they know not of. Daniel has

been freed from foster care and endless facilities

that seemed to warehouse children, instead of

celebrating their individual needs as a child, by

graciously becoming of age and releasing himself

from "the system". Daniel begins to reminisce

on how far and in between days of thanksgiving

poured from his spirit in prayer. "Thank you, Jesus,

for my fresh start." "And . . . if you don't mind me

saying so, Lord, help me to get it right this time."

Daniel chuckled. "I know that I have walked away

from a lot of my blessings and from people who

genuinely cared for me." Daniel explained to God.

"I just didn't want Gabby to be left alone, Lord."

"She really needs me." "Lord, I just want to be a

blessing to someone else that is worse off than

me." "In Jesus' name I pray." "Amen." Daniel had

finished his special prayer for his best friend.

Gabby was standing outside of his bedroom door

as she listened in on his prayer. This prayer had

detoured Gabby from her usual goodnight prayer

with Daniel.

Gabrielle has found a life on the streets to be

more intriguing, than that of, the nature of knowing

first hand, about sweat shops and work houses

that left bruises and scars that were separated by

time and space, but were attached to a place in her

spirit that housed a glimpse of her "eternity". Gabby

and Daniel were soul mates. Their spirits were

bound for connection long before "the system"

ever streamed into their destiny. The relationship

between Gabby and Daniel was no secret to "the

system". After her undefined motives, for countless

numbers of disappearing acts, the only way of

securely confining her, was to facilitate her with

Daniel's presence.

"Hey, kiddo." "You must have been pretty tired

last night," Daniel said. "What do you mean?"

Gabby replied. "Well, we pray together every night

but last night you never showed up." "I went to your

bedroom to look in on you but you were already

fast asleep." Daniel responded. "Yeah, sorry about

that." Gabby stated. "I just figured since you were

leaving, I should get used to praying by myself and

for myself." Gabby explained. "I guess you're right."

"But I won't be far away and I will come to visit."

Daniel announced to Gabby. "One day I am going

to get you out of here." "Look at me, Gabby." "I

have always kept my word to you." "Someday . . .

soon, you're coming home with me." "You're my

best friend, Gabby." Daniel explained passionately.

"Yeah, I know . . . soul mates." "I get it, alright?" "I

have to go to school now." "See you around, okay?"

Gabby responded in anger. "Gabby, can I have a

hug?" Daniel asked. Gabrielle looks at Daniel with

tears in her eyes, ignores his request, and walks

away.

Daniel fought hard to regain his composure and

left the facility with a duffle bag, a laptop, and a

sealed folder full of charted information from the

time of his birth. He was looking at his laptop in

total frustration. Suddenly, there was a loud thump

under his feet. He realized a bag had fallen to the

ground in the vicinity of his own belongings. Oh

no...it was not just any bag. There was Gabby standing

right next to him. Gabrielle's head was lowered

in sadness and confusion. She had no idea what

Daniel's response would be when he realized that

she had left school to be with him. However, it was

clear that she had no problem tenaciously inquiring

about the journey that could endanger his future and

the nature of her destiny.

Daniel could not fathom the idea of walking into

that place of "eternity" without Gabby. However, he

knew he had a responsibility to make her understand

that Heaven's Secret Garden could not be that place

in time that they have always dreamed of, if they

walked into their "level of eternity" in survival mode,

constantly running from "the system". Together,

they braved one last storm as the downpour of rain

demonstrated Gabrielle's tears. Enduring the hustle

and bustle of the downtown bus terminal, Daniel

and Gabrielle graciously redeemed the time by

writing one last entry in each of their journals before

exchanging them with one another. He kissed her

on her forehead and quietly walked away. Shortly

after reading her first journal entry, Daniel knew

returning Gabrielle to the facility was the right thing

to do. The journey that is required of them both

to enter "Heaven's Secret Garden" would be

worth the wait as he continues to read the journal

she had left in his charge.

Heaven's Secret Garden

Day of Emancipation

I can do all things through Christ which strengthens me. Philippians 4:13

The Challenge(s):

_____
_____
_____
_____
_____
_____
_____
_____
_____
_____
_____
_____
_____
_____
_____
_____
_____
_____
_____
_____
_____
_____
_____
_____
_____
_____
_____
_____
_____
_____Philippians 4:13

Heaven's Secret Garden

I can do all things through Christ which strengthens me. Philippians 4:13

The Experience(s):

_____
_____
_____
_____
_____
_____
_____
_____
_____
_____
_____
_____
_____
_____
_____
_____
_____
_____
_____
_____
_____
_____
_____
_____
_____
_____
_____
_____
_____
_____
_____
_____
_____
_____Philippians 4:13

Heaven's Secret Garden

I can do all things through Christ which strengthens me. Philippians 4:13

The Victory:

_____
_____
_____
_____
_____
_____
_____
_____
_____
_____
_____
_____
_____
_____
_____
_____
_____
_____
_____
_____
_____
_____
_____
_____
_____
_____
_____
_____
_____
_____
_____
_____Philippians 4:13

Heaven's Secret Garden

I can do all things through Christ which strengthens me. Philippians 4:13

Scripture(s) and Prayer(s): That Brought Healing and Strength to Your Experience

_____

_____

_____

_____

_____

_____

_____

_____

_____

_____

_____

_____

_____

_____

_____

_____

_____

_____

_____

_____

_____

_____

_____

_____

_____

_____

_____

_____

_____

_____

_____

_____

_____

_____Philippians 4:13

HEAVEN'S SECRET GARDEN:

LADY TURQUOISE

Tina, a young lady with an extraordinary gift to see

spirits from the other side has begun preparations to

take a cruise. She will be going with her significant

other. Tina was hoping to get away from her sometimes

tormenting, yet secretive lifestyle of being a spiritual

guide when she went on this cruise, but listen closely

as she makes her way to "Heaven's Secret Garden".

Tina ends her conversation with her best friend

named Miracle.

"I have to go . . . call me on the house phone if you

need anything." "I'll call you with my new cell phone

number later," Tina said.

"Alright." "Hey, I know this has been really hard

on you." Miracle stated supportively in Tina's time of

need. "So, have a great time on the cruise." "And don't

worry about this place." "Everyone will be just fine." "Even those spirits that you communicate with, okay?" They both laughed. "Thanks", said Tina.

Tina packs for the cruise and is now boarding the ship. The ship sets sail. She leans over towards the rails of the ship. Then she looks up to see this beautiful waterfall with a rainbow crossing the waters. Tina felt a strange tap on her shoulder. She looks and sees this lady dressed in turquoise clothing.

Tina said, "Oh my . . . you frightened me." But the lady, in turquoise clothing, just disappeared into the cool breeze as was the waterfall, with the rainbow. Tina runs to find her companion who came with her on the ship. Immediately she began rambling on about how the lady in the turquoise dress . . .

"Wait a minute." "Didn't we take this trip to get

away from all of that?" Tina's companion stated

angrily. "Yes, but . . ." she rambled.

"But nothing." "No more ghosts and that's final",

he said. Tina looks saddened by the response. "I'm

sorry." "I just wanted this trip to be perfect." "You've

been through so much. He was alarmed by the look

in her eyes and felt the need to explain his response.

"I came really close to losing you and . . ." he went on

to say.

"Please if you want to pursue this when we get

back home, that's fine."

"But not here, okay? Not here." Tina's companion

stated seriously.

"Let's get something to eat", he said.

"No, I'm not very hungry." Tina responded.

"Look, there are lots of things on this ship that we can do." "Let's just take a little tour until you get your appetite back", he said.

"No, you go ahead." "I just want to go back to the cabin and rest." Tina replied. "That's fine." "I'll walk you back", he gently answered. Tina lays down on the bed for a nap and Lady Turquoise appears to her in a dream. "Who are you?" "Why are you here?" Tina yelled fearfully.

Lady Turquoise addresses her. "I knew you were coming." "The dancing hands of the waterfalls showed me your face." "I have been following your presence all the way up the mainstream." Lady Turquoise told her. "Your fears are blocking me."

"Please don't be afraid." The spirit begged. "I don't want to intrude." "I forced my way into your dreams because you wouldn't let me into your world." "Into your spirit . . ." she explained further. "Yes, I need to show you something." "But only from within, you see." "It's the only way I can go with you . . . I mean the only way you can see", explained Lady Turquoise.

"See what?" "I need to be with you when your ship turns back."

Someone shakes Tina outside of her dreams. She wakes up in a panic. "Hey, it's okay." "It's just me." Her companion exclaimed. "What's going on?" Her companion said in an investing voice. She plays it off as though she is not troubled. They went to dinner and listened to poetic expressions. Suddenly it's like the atmosphere just changed to suit what Tina was experiencing on the ship. She recognized that Lady Turquoise had somehow swept her into her world.

"Next we will have poetic expressions by Lady Turquoise." The hostess said to the small crowd in the audience. Tina immediately jumps up and runs out.

"Tina," he shouted. Tina's companion meets her by the upper deck.

"She was there." "She's trying to tell me something." Tina shouted.

Tina was so hysterical that she simply passed out as she tried to explain to her companion. He picked Tina up and carried her back to the cabin. The next morning the ship hit land. Tina and her companion walked on the shoreline of Heaven's Secret Garden and there was no sign of Lady Turquoise. It was a normal day and all was well. That is, until it was time to set sail. Everyone had boarded the ship. When Tina came back to her cabin with her companion, there was written with turquoise paint bleeding down the walls of her cabin, a poem about Lady

Turquoise. Her companion went ballistic. He started

ranting and raving about what this was doing to Tina.

"Come on, we're going to see the captain." He told

her. "No, she's not going to stop . . ." Tina told him.

"I have to do this."

"Do what?" Her companion asked abruptly.

"Just leave . . ." she said angrily.

"I'm not going to leave you." Her companion replied.

"You have to." Tina pleaded. "She won't come if you

don't leave." "Who?" "I don't understand." "What

is going on?" Her companion questioned frantically.

"You've never kept anything from me before." "Why

are you shutting me out now?" He wanted to know.

"I'm not." Look, this isn't about you." "I'll explain

everything later." "I promise." Tina affirmed. "Just let

me confront her alone."

"Fine." "I'm going to the captain about this mess

on the walls." "No, I'll wait outside the door if you

need me." "Then we'll go to the captain together."

He insisted. "Lady Turquoise, you come out here right

now." She stated aggressively. "Now I know you wrote

this on the walls." "It's okay." "I'm ready to listen." Tina

told her. There was a faint voice in the background. "I

don't want your ears," she said softly. Then with a

demonic voice she screams out, "I want your . . ."

Her companion runs into the cabin. "Are you

okay?"

"No," she cries.

"I just wanted to help her." "She's stuck and she

needs to cross over before . . ." she couldn't begin to

explain.

Her mate calms her down and they went to see the

captain. The captain talks to them and assures them

that their trip will no longer be interrupted. "We'll

post one of our men at your door." The captain told

them.

"Thank you, captain." They both said in a monotone

voice.

Tina pondered all night on ways to help Lady

Turquoise and finally she thought of a way. The ship

went ashore to its next destination where Tina and

her companion went to dinner. There was a beautiful

waterfall behind the outside café. It was open mic

night and Tina decided to participate to help Lady

Turquoise cross over. She read a spoken word entitled

Understanding Lady Turquoise through the Divine

Eyes of Morning Glory.

Lady Turquoise suffered violence at the hands

of someone she mistakenly put her trust in. But

her aggressor turned out to be her blessing, if

you will. She was not very respected in society

before her untimely passing over. The history of

her past seemed to follow her even after her days

of repentance. She was a lady of African decent.

However, she did appear to be racially mixed. Lady

Turquoise communicated with me. She stated that

though being tossed out of a boat, falling over the

edge of a waterfall, captured by the spur of a cave,

and entering into a divine state of mind, was not

built on her hope for her life, she is thankful that

God is mindful of her. She held onto everything

that surrounded her, making all that she saw an

extension of her faith. An endless dancing of

the water and the waterfalls before her took her

anywhere that she wanted to go; the stones that

surrounded her became her sanctuary and were

indeed her key connection to her view of Heaven.

With every hope of being delivered, she began

collecting these yellow and turquoise stones that

seemed to surround her on the outskirts of the

cave. She did, of course, as anyone, in her situation

would, grow weary and tired. She began finding

security in the rocks below, as they constantly

wooed her with what one would have thought of

as being "unfeigned imaginings" of "Showers of

Blessings". Until she was at, what she thought was

the ending of her faith, suddenly ushered her into

her fate. She looked at the stones behind her as

she cleaved to the edge of the waterfall, listening

to the rocks calling out to her. Instantly, the earth

was quieted, and her Savior had spoken . . .

I have preserved you for such a time as this. Listen,

my child, the cave is your covering, the waterfall is

my tears, and the stones represent the pearls I have

waiting for you on the other side. She stared at the

stones and asked, "But how can these little stones

save me." He simply stated would faith be faith if you

could see it? Remember, faith is the substance of

things hoped for, the evidence of things not seen.

Let me show you a change of scenery. Suddenly, the

hand of God reached down and grabbed the stones.

He had replaced them with a seashell of turquoise

pearls. She then stated, but . . . my Lord, if thou art

so mighty and thy hands are so strong, why not just

pick me up and carry me away. He stated that in all

of my glory you have yet to praise me and honor

my very presence. But the rocks, knew enough

to start singing "Showers of Blessings", before I

even showed my face. No, my child, picking you up

would be too easy. But more than reverencing my

name, I want you to know that you have a choice.

To every trial, there is a lesson to be learned and perhaps passed on. Most importantly, I need you to understand that this is not where your faith ends, but where the true testing of your faith begins.

So she hardened not her heart, and gave ear unto His words. When her mind was changed, she saw dancing hands on the other side of the waterfall. She grabbed her turquoise pearls and reached for the dancing hands, as far as her faith would take her, immediately being ushered into a new dimension. She looked at her pearls, which were no longer turquoise, but were so transformed into a pearly white. When she was done, she received a standing ovation. She walked off of the stage and grabbed her companion's hand. They went behind the café to the waterfalls, where she saw Lady Turquoise.

"How did you know what happened to me?" Lady

Turquoise asked.

"I don't know." "It's like our spirits just connected

after I saw the handwriting on the walls." Tina stated.

"There were people I never got to say good-bye

to." "Money matters I never took care of you know."

"Here's the number of my lawyer." "Tell him what

you know and give this to him." "It's all I had before

the . . ."

"He'll know that I'm not coming back when you

show it to him." Lady Turquoise expressed. Then the

rainbow appeared. "Who was it that hurt you,

Lady Turquoise?" her companion asked.

"It doesn't matter anymore."

"They did me a favor by releasing me." "I am free now."

"I can move on." "Where is that music coming from?"

Lady Turquoise asked. "They are the angels of Heaven's

Secret Garden." "It is there way of calling you home."

Tina stated full of emotion and endless tears.

The rainbow disappeared and a yellowish-gold

illumination glared off of the waterfall.

"Wow, it's more beautiful than I have ever

imagined." "I have to go." "I just needed someone to

know." "See you on the other side." Lady Turquoise

whispered. As her turquoise spirit merged into the

yellowish-gold illumination, she dissipated invisibly

into the waterfall. Tina's companion held her tightly

and before she could respond to his strong grip, these

white pearls flew out right into her hands, like the

wings of an unannounced angel. In the end, Tina's

companion asked for her hand in marriage. She gladly

accepts the proposal. As she walked down the aisle,

on her wedding day, in her white pearls, she knew

that Lady Turquoise was somewhere in the midst

of the blessed event. Tina gazed up into the bright,

blue sky and she was mesmerized by an illuminating

rainbow that covered her as the ceremony reached

its end. In fact, Tina will even go so far as to say, that

Lady Turquoise had found her way into her newfound

destiny through her at the very moment.

Heaven's Secret Garden

Lady Turquoise

I can do all things through Christ which strengthens me. Philippians 4:13

The Challenge(s):

_____
_____
_____
_____
_____
_____
_____
_____
_____
_____
_____
_____
_____
_____
_____
_____
_____
_____
_____
_____
_____
_____
_____
_____
_____
_____
_____
_____
_____
_____
_____Philippians 4:13

Heaven's Secret Garden

I can do all things through Christ which strengthens me. Philippians 4:13

The Experience(s):

_____
_____
_____
_____
_____
_____
_____
_____
_____
_____
_____
_____
_____
_____
_____
_____
_____
_____
_____
_____
_____
_____
_____
_____
_____
_____
_____
_____
_____
_____
_____
_____Philippians 4:13

Heaven's Secret Garden

I can do all things through Christ which strengthens me. Philippians 4:13

The Victory:

_____

_____

_____

_____

_____

_____

_____

_____

_____

_____

_____

_____

_____

_____

_____

_____

_____

_____

_____

_____

_____

_____

_____

_____

_____

_____

_____

_____

_____

_____

_____

_____

_____

_____Philippians 4:13

Heaven's Secret Garden

I can do all things through Christ which strengthens me. Philippians 4:13

Scripture(s) and Prayer(s): That Brought Healing and Strength to Your Experience

_____
_____
_____
_____
_____
_____
_____
_____
_____
_____
_____
_____
_____
_____
_____
_____
_____
_____
_____
_____
_____
_____
_____
_____
_____
_____
_____
_____
_____
_____
_____
_____
_____
_____Philippians 4:13

HEAVEN'S SECRET GARDEN:

MIXED SIGNALS

HSG International is proceeding with

weekly reviews of the portal strength in portal one of

Heaven's Secret Garden. Meanwhile, trouble awaits.

Shields and defenses are down. Communication

modules in Heaven's Secret Garden have been giving

off mixed signals in their efforts to pass through

the portal. Could there be an enemy in the camp or

perhaps a new breed of life-forms with a language

barrier they have not explored.

This is Ambassador CX-2 reporting for assignment

in portal one, Sir. I'm trying to pass through but

I'm getting mixed signals. It's like two portals in one.

What do I do?

Stand still . . .

Okay. I am doing that. Now what, sir?

Which portal has a stronger magnetic pull?

The one in the middle but...

Which one speaks loudest into your spirit?

The outer portal . . . it's like I'm being pulled into

two different dimensions.

Hold on one minute . . . Commander, this is

Ambassador CX-2 of HSG International Airbase.

Report your status CX-2 . . .

Sir, we have a transmitter down.

One of my members on the HSG spiritual

navigator received the go ahead to enter a portal.

But the HSG member was targeted by a wheel

within a wheel.

CX-2 does the wheel that's within the wheel

coincide with the original assignment.

That's unknown at this time, sir. My HSG member

lost all connections with the original target of the

base assignment upon entering the first portal.

I'm getting a read back on that transmitter.

No report of any damage in portal one or three.

This could be a trick. Pull your HSG member out.

But sir . . .

Swap him out for one of the HSG robotic

members. Just in case, your HSG member has

been tagged by an illegal in between the portals

gravitational pull. Yes, Sir. Right away, Sir.

HSG member, this is Ambassador CX-2 reporting.

Abort mission . . . step into the outer portal. I'm sending

an HSG robotic member in to investigate this matter.

Advise the HSG robotic member to maintain position,

report all findings, and check all communication

modules upon entering the quadrant. HSG member,

are you hurt?

No, Sir.

Even so, report to sick bay . . . and do not forget to

decontaminate before your report back to duty.

Yes, Sir. Thank you, Sir. Affirmative.

Back to HSG Commander there is a regime trying to

make contact.

Mayday, mayday, Tabernacle down . . .

Tabernacle what's your location?

I repeat state your location?

This is the commander in chief of

HSG International Airbase, do you read?

Signal breaking up

We were on route . . .

From where?

Quadrant three, portal one.

We have tracked you on our radar beam.

Where are we?

You are in quadrant nine, portal six.

State your damage.

We are manually assessing the damage now.

That report is unconfirmed, Sir.

There is an unidentified species on this quadrant

that you are to stay clear of. Do you read?

That's affirmative, commander.

Shut down everything but your communication

modules until we arrive to access any outer core

damage.

That's affirmative. Thanks commander.

Approaching . . . the damage is astronomical. Get

them out of there immediately. Tag everything that

comes on board. Make sure they go directly to sick bay

and there I will meet you. Make sure they understand

that all belongings must be left behind. Naked they

entered the world, naked they must return . . .

Tell them that their essential needs shall be met

accordingly.

CX-7, what is your location?

Prayer chambers, Sir.

Report to the altar of Sacrifice, right away.

Affirmative.

CX-7 reporting, Sir.

Your sacrifice has been noted and deemed

acceptable. I have an assignment for you.

There is a new regime in sick bay.

Our records show that they are strong in numbers

but weak in an area that they may find beneficial. They

have weak communicational skills. However, they do

move to the operative beat of numeric equations.

They are not even aware of

their problem-solving capabilities. If we tag them

accordingly, we can generate a divine order to open

portals that have been closed for centuries. We are

in need of a hidden quadrant. In our efforts to rescue

the Tabernacle regime, we have run the risk of being

tagged and identified to outside forces. These outside

forces have extraordinary warfare abilities.

But sir, we are trained to conquer . . . I mean we

are an indestructible regime.

Very true, commander. But you fail to understand that

we have on board thousands of species from an alliance

that we have yet to fully understand. We did not rescue

them only to put them in further danger. Our initial goal

is to learn as much as we can about the regime, take

them to their original location, or find out more about

their original mission and possibly combine forces

and live peacefully in a new dimension, creating more

quadrants, and open new portals leading to possibly

greater hidden dimensions in Heaven's Secret Garden.

Affirmative, sir. This is Ambassador CX-2 reporting

to sick bay. I will have all reports on your desk and ready for review immediately.

Affirmative. Thank you, Ambassador CX-2. You are dismissed.

This is Heaven's Secret Garden Rescue Mission reporting for duty, sir.

Commander CX-7 is now in a meeting with the commanders of the new regime aboard HSG International. I now introduce to you the power and range of a level of servitude, ladies and gentlemen that we are required to reach in our spirit. This is not to thrust our power of authority into new galaxies that await us. This is being done to establish a new covenant of peace and unity between the two as we rebuild the hope of a new earth where we can all be free like we once were before the war tides swept over our native lands and destroyed our homes. This has become a new energy source . . . a newly modified language we

are now pursuing in new realms of Heaven's Secret

Garden. Let us welcome aboard this regime with open

arms of love and appreciation for their existence in the

heavens we intend to explore in the days to come.

It is my understanding that you are providing the

essential needs for me and my people, while we are

on board.

That's affirmative.

Then we are from this moment on in full submission

to the needs of your regime.

We can be helpers one to another. Our children

lack in an area that your people are secure in. We

need math teachers . . . numerically, they

struggle. It is for that cause that we are significantly

low in numbers.

Say no more. I will assign the regimes best

professors to complete the task. We will not let you

down, sir. Is that all commander?

That will be all at this time. Thank you.

They bow their heads in agreement. HSG Robotic

team on to the next dimension of glory. Yes, sir.

And they proceeded into a new horizon of

cyber galactic sunsets.

What new dimension now awaits this crew?

I would say only time will tell, but everybody

knows that Heaven's Secret Garden is timeless.

Heaven's Secret Garden

Mixed Signals

I can do all things through Christ which strengthens me. Philippians 4:13

The Challenge(s):

_____
_____
_____
_____
_____
_____
_____
_____
_____
_____
_____
_____
_____
_____
_____
_____
_____
_____
_____
_____
_____
_____
_____
_____
_____
_____
_____
_____
_____
_____
_____
_____Philippians 4:13

Heaven's Secret Garden

I can do all things through Christ which strengthens me. Philippians 4:13

The Experience(s):

_____
_____
_____
_____
_____
_____
_____
_____
_____
_____
_____
_____
_____
_____
_____
_____
_____
_____
_____
_____
_____
_____
_____
_____
_____
_____
_____
_____
_____
_____
_____Philippians 4:13

Heaven's Secret Garden

I can do all things through Christ which strengthens me. Philippians 4:13

The Victory:

_____
_____
_____
_____
_____
_____
_____
_____
_____
_____
_____
_____
_____
_____
_____
_____
_____
_____
_____
_____
_____
_____
_____
_____
_____
_____
_____
_____
_____
_____
_____
_____
_____Philippians 4:13

Heaven's Secret Garden

I can do all things through Christ which strengthens me. Philippians 4:13

Scripture(s) and Prayer(s): That Brought Healing and Strength to Your Experience

_____

_____

_____

_____

_____

_____

_____

_____

_____

_____

_____

_____

_____

_____

_____

_____

_____

_____

_____

_____

_____

_____

_____

_____

_____

_____

_____

_____

_____

_____

_____

_____Philippians 4:13

Heaven's Secret Garden

I can do all things through Christ which strengthens me. Philippians 4:13

Congratulations

Awarded To: _____

From: Heaven's Secret Garden

This certifies that you can do all things
through Christ which strengthens you.

Philippians 4:13

Heaven's Secret Garden commends you
for taking the first step which is believing
in God and believing in yourself. However,
we would like to encourage you to take the
next step which is establishing your
salvation in the Lord Jesus Christ. This
will allow you to stay in relationship with
the One who can take you on your
own personal journey…Jesus Christ.
Romans 10 will help you gain access
into the heart of God. The Word of God
is an open door to all that Jesus Christ
has in store for you. We pray that you
have been refreshed in *Heaven's Secret Garden.*

Made in the USA
Columbia, SC
29 September 2018